KT-501-304

RAINBOW
magic®
The Green Fairies

ORCHARD BOOKS
338 Euston Road, London NW1 3BH
Orchard Books Australia
Level 17/207 Kent Street, Sydney, NSW 2000
A Paperback Original

First published in 2009 by Orchard Books.

A CIP catalogue record for this book is available
from the British Library.

ISBN 978 1 40830 476 1
1 3 5 7 9 10 8 6 4 2

Printed in Great Britain

The paper and board used in this paperback are natural recyclable
products made from wood grown in sustainable forests. The
manufacturing processes conform to the environmental regulations
of the country of origin.

Orchard Books is a division of Hachette Children's Books,
an Hachette UK company

www.hachette.co.uk

Edie the Garden Fairy

by Daisy Meadows

www.rainbowmagic.co.uk

The Fairyland Palace
River Rapids
Seabury
Car Ferry
Rainforest

Jack Frost's Ice Castle
Rainspell Island
Wildlife Garden
Lake
Cottage
Harbour
Beach
The Coral Reef
Ice Cap

The fairies must be in a dream
If they think they can be called 'green'.
My goblin servants are definitely greenest
And I, of course, am by far the meanest.

Seven fairies out to save the Earth?
This idea fills me full of mirth!
I'm sure the world has had enough
Of fairy magic and all that stuff.

So I'm going to steal the fairies' wands
And send them into human lands.
The fairies will think all is lost
Defeated again, by me, Jack Frost!

Contents

Project Green

"It's another lovely day, Kirsty!" Rachel exclaimed happily as she and her best friend, Kirsty Tate, hurried along the winding country lane. The blue sky above them was dotted with fluffy white clouds, and the sun was warm on their faces. "Isn't Rainspell Island just the most *magical* place?"

"I can't think of anywhere else I'd rather go on holiday," Kirsty replied, gazing over the lush green fields. The aquamarine sea sparkled in the distance and seagulls wheeled through the crisp, salty air.

The Tates and the Walkers had arrived on the island three days ago to spend the autumn half-term week there.

"It's great that we're helping to keep Rainspell clean and beautiful, isn't it, Rachel?" Kirsty added. "Do you have the leaflet that came yesterday?"

Rachel pulled the leaflet out of her pocket. *Project Green* was written at the top, and underneath it read:

Would YOU like to help the Rainspell Gardening Club make a NEW garden out of an area of disused land? Then please join us at our site in Butterfly Lane tomorrow. Wear old clothes!

"I'm glad we decided to volunteer," Kirsty said, as they studied the leaflet. "We might have our friends the Green Fairies to help us with the environment, but we humans have to do our bit, too!"

Rachel nodded. Rainspell Island was a very special place because it was where she and Kirsty had first become good friends with the fairies. Since then the girls had had many magical, amazing adventures while helping the fairies to outwit cold, sly Jack Frost and his goblin servants.

But now it was Rachel and Kirsty's turn to ask the fairies for help. When the girls had arrived on Rainspell Island, they'd been shocked to see lots of litter strewn around the golden beach, so they'd asked the king and queen of Fairyland to help clean up the human world with fairy magic. King Oberon and Queen Titania had decided that seven fairies currently in training would become the Green Fairies. These fairies would help Rachel and Kirsty make the world a greener place. If the Green Fairies were successful, they would become fully-fledged, permanent fairies.

But just as the Fairyland Wand ceremony was about to begin, the goblins had stolen the wands that were to be presented to the Green Fairies.

Then Jack Frost's icy spell had immediately sent the goblins and wands spinning away into the human world to hide. Jack Frost was determined not to help the world become greener, but Rachel and Kirsty were equally determined to make sure all seven of the Green Fairies got their wands back from the goblins. Then, together, they could carry on the task of helping the world to become a cleaner, greener place.

"We've made a good start," Rachel said cheerfully. "We've already tracked down Nicole the Beach Fairy's wand, and Isabella the Air Fairy's, too."

"But it's a bit scary to think that there are *five* more goblins running around with fairy wands!" Kirsty frowned. "I hope we find them soon, so that the Green Fairies can get on with the job of helping to clean up our world."

"Remember what Queen Titania said though," Rachel reminded her. "Fairy magic isn't powerful enough to fix all the problems of the environment on its own. We humans have to help too!"

"I know." Kirsty nodded. "We must be very close to the *Project Green* area, now, Rachel," she said, looking around.

The girls walked on. At the bottom of Butterfly Lane they came to a large, open area of wasteland. Rachel and Kirsty could see several people milling about. Some were collecting up rubbish that had been dumped, and carting it away in wheelbarrows. The girls could see old sofas, rusty bicycles and broken toys among the junk. Some volunteers were pulling up weeds and digging over the soil. Meanwhile, others were unloading tools and plants from the backs of trucks.

"There's lots to do," Rachel whispered to Kirsty, "This doesn't look like a garden at all, yet!"

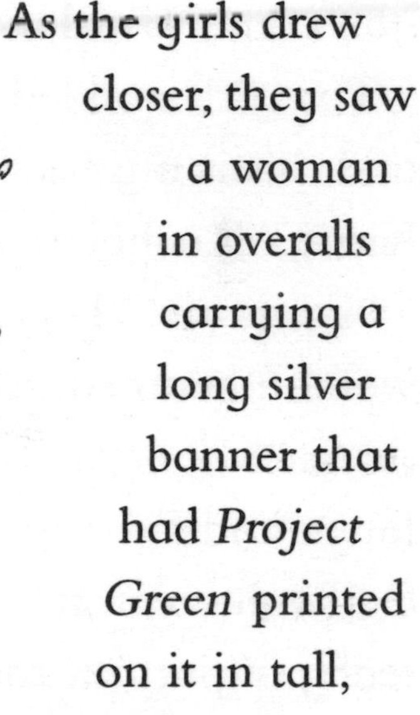

As the girls drew closer, they saw a woman in overalls carrying a long silver banner that had *Project Green* printed on it in tall, emerald-green letters.

The woman began trying to hang the banner over a big wooden arch at the entrance to the wasteland, but it was so long, she got tangled up in it. Rachel and Kirsty rushed to help.

"Oh, thank you!" the woman said breathlessly as the girls helped her to drape the banner over the arch. "Have you come to volunteer?"

The girls nodded eagerly. "I'm Rachel and this is my friend, Kirsty," Rachel explained.

"Fantastic!" The woman beamed at them. "My name's Janet, and I'm the lead volunteer. It's really important that we get the garden set up as soon as possible because..." Janet glanced anxiously at her watch. "In a very short time, the builders and their diggers are arriving to turn this space into a car park!"

"That's terrible!" Kirsty gasped.

"We've been learning at school how important green spaces are," Rachel added.

"Yes, we need parks for people to enjoy, not more *car* parks!" Janet said firmly. "The only person with the power to stop the builders is the mayor of Rainspell Island himself. We've explained to the mayor that we want to show him how well this space would work as a garden – and he's promised to come along in one hour to see for himself."

"Only one hour!" Rachel exclaimed. "That doesn't give us much time."

"How can we help?" asked Kirsty.

"See the fields around the wasteland?" Janet pointed at the fields that bordered the land on two sides. "You can dig holes and plant saplings around the edges of the garden. Then, when the trees have grown, they'll help to protect the space from wind and rain. Come on, I'll find you some spades."

Rachel and Kirsty followed Janet across the wasteland. More volunteers were arriving all the time, and there was a buzz of activity as everyone got down to work.

"Start over there at the corner of the field, and make sure you space the holes out evenly," Janet told the girls as she handed them a spade each. "Here are the saplings. We have oak, beech and ash. If you have any problems, come and find me." And with a quick smile, Janet dashed off to welcome a new group of volunteers.

Rachel and Kirsty each collected an armload of tiny saplings and then headed off towards the edge of the wasteland. Suddenly, without any warning, the saplings in Rachel's arms began to tremble slightly, tickling her nose.

Rachel gave a gasp. She was longing to scratch the tip of her nose, but her arms were full.

"Oh, Kirsty, help!" she called. "The saplings are tickling my nose. I think I'm going to sneeze, and then I might drop everything!"

Kirsty immediately put her own saplings down and dashed over to Rachel. Her friend was twitching her nose in a desperate effort to stop herself from sneezing. Quickly, Kirsty took the saplings from Rachel. She peered closely at the tiny trees, and then gave a cry of delight.

"Oh, that's better!" Rachel sighed with relief, rubbing her nose vigorously. "But why were the saplings shaking like that, Kirsty?"

Kirsty laughed. "Try and guess!"

"Is there a spider or a bumble-bee hiding in there?" asked Rachel.

"No, but we *have* seen these creatures before, and they have shimmery wings!" Kirsty replied, her eyes twinkling.

"A butterfly?" Rachel guessed. "We *are* in Butterfly Lane, after all."

Kirsty shook her head. She laid the saplings on the ground and beckoned to Rachel to look more closely. Once again the saplings quivered and trembled – and then a glittering fairy danced out from among the branches!

Garden Magic!

The fairy hovered in front of Rachel and Kirsty, a huge smile on her face. She wore a pretty blue sun-dress, a pink hat, and cute pink and white polka-dot wellies. She carried a straw basket in her hand. "Girls, remember me?" she said. "I'm Edie the Garden Fairy!"

"Hello again, Edie," Rachel laughed.

"And if you're here, then that means your wand is close by!" Kirsty said eagerly.

Edie nodded. "Yes, and I need your help to get it back, girls," she replied. "As you know, I don't have much magic of my own, as I'm still in training.

Getting my wand back will give me a magical boost, and then I'll be able to start looking after gardens everywhere!"

"We'd love to help, Edie," Kirsty explained, "But we've promised to plant all these saplings."

"We have to make this space look green and beautiful before the mayor arrives, otherwise it'll be turned into a car park!" Rachel added.

Edie looked horrified. "Girls, we can work on the garden *and* look for my wand," she assured them. "Green spaces are *so* important. I'll help you plant the saplings, and we can keep a look-out for the goblin who has my wand at the same time. I just know he's around here somewhere!"

The girls were right at the edge of the garden away from the other volunteers, but Edie stayed hidden among the saplings, just to be on the safe side. Meanwhile Kirsty began digging holes, pacing the distance between each one carefully. Rachel followed behind her, planting the saplings.

"You could plant them in groups of three," Edie suggested, peeping out to watch. "Oak, then beech, then ash and so on."

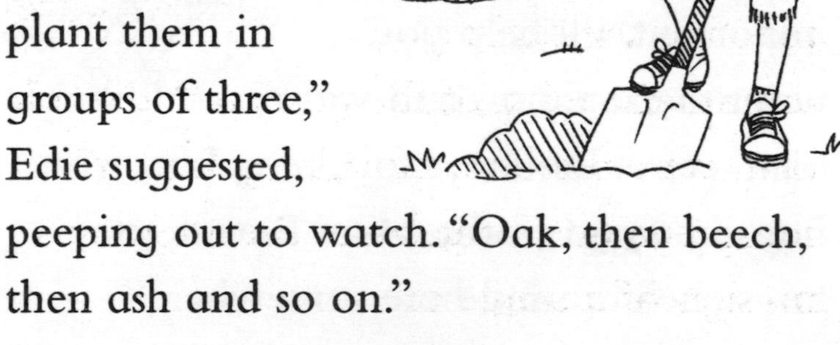

"Good idea," Kirsty agreed, beginning to dig another hole. "Oh!" she panted, "the earth's really hard here!"

Edie snapped her fingers and a few sparkles of fairy magic drifted down onto the ground. Kirsty tried again, and this time her spade slid smoothly into the earth.

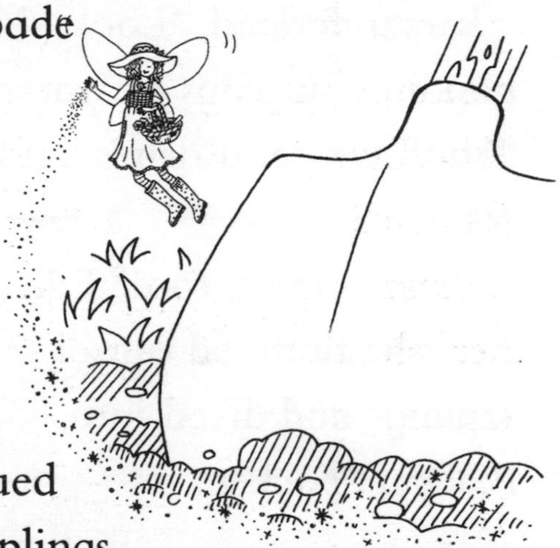

"Thanks, Edie," she laughed.

Kirsty and Rachel continued planting the saplings around the edge of the garden. Although they were working hard, they kept a sharp eye out for goblins. But there was no sign of a single one.

"We've almost finished planting these two sides now," Rachel said with satisfaction. She turned and glanced over to where the other volunteers were hard at work. "The garden's starting to look lots better, isn't it?"

Kirsty nodded. "Look, there's someone handing out cups of water," she said. "Shall we get a drink before we finish off here?"

"I'm coming too!" Edie whispered. And she fluttered out of the saplings and dived into Rachel's pocket.

The girls walked across the garden, stopping to take a look at the various projects the other volunteers were working on.

"Hi, girls," called Janet, who was planting rows of sweet-scented lavender bushes. "We're making mini-gardens. Come and see!"

Rachel and Kirsty hurried over. One of the mini-gardens was full of herbs, planted in circular beds, and another was full of beautiful, fragrant shrubs with pink, white and purple flowers.

"And that one's a wild flower garden," Janet explained, pointing at the plot next to hers where people were planting poppies, daisies and cornflowers. "We've chosen plants that attract wildlife because we want this garden to be a place for people *and* animals to enjoy."

Kirsty turned as a flash of russet-brown caught her eye.

"I think it's working already!" she laughed, pointing across the garden.

Rachel, Janet and the others turned just in time to see a fox dart between the piles of junk. They all grinned.

"This will be a perfect place for foxes and other wildlife!" Edie whispered, popping out of Rachel's pocket. The girls had collected their drinks and were heading back to finish planting the saplings.

"Next time we come back to Rainspell Island, everything will have grown a little more," Kirsty said. "It'll be brilliant to know that we helped to plant the garden, Rachel!"

"As long as the gardening club can convince the mayor to cancel the car park," Rachel pointed out with a sigh. Suddenly she gave a gasp of horror. "Kirsty, look at our saplings!"

Kirsty cried out in surprise as she stared at the trees they'd planted.

Half the saplings had been pulled from the earth, and now lay limply on the ground!

Rachel knelt down and picked up one of the saplings.

"Maybe the mini-gardens are working too well already!" she suggested. "Perhaps an animal has come along and dug them up."

"Could be," Edie agreed. "But they must be replanted quickly or they'll die."

She took a quick glance around, and then snapped her fingers. A faint mist of fairy dust surrounded the saplings, and when it cleared, the girls were relieved to see that they were all neatly planted in the holes again.

"Thanks, Edie," they chorused.

"Oh, no!" someone yelled behind them.

Edie quickly hid in Rachel's pocket again. The girls spun round, hearts pounding, as they heard other shouts of amazement. Had someone spotted the tiny fairy?

Janet was looking upset, so the girls rushed over to her.

"What's happened, Janet?" Rachel asked.

"Everything's going wrong!" Janet sighed. "Someonc has uprooted one of the big butterfly bushes we planted, *and* upended a big bag of flower seeds on the floor!"

In the middle of the garden, Rachel and Kirsty could see a big shrub with purple flowers lying on its side, its roots in the air beside a pile of tiny brown seeds. A broken old chair and a couple of rusty tools lay next to them.

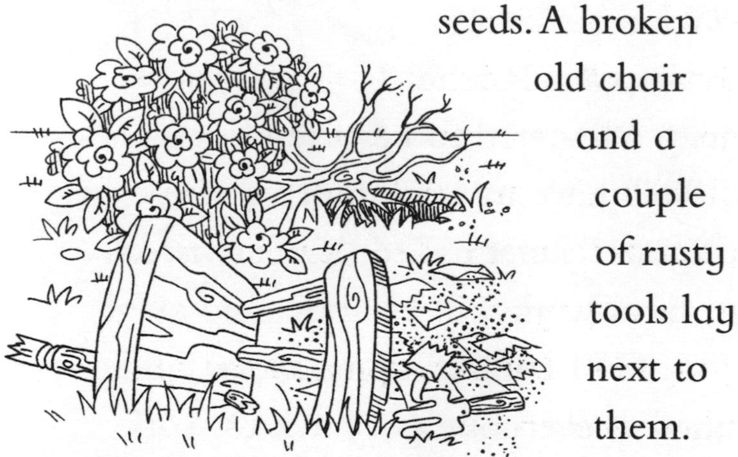

"And someone's moving all the junk around too!" Janet went on crossly. "Those things were on the rubbish pile, and now they're back in the garden!" She shook her head sadly. "At this rate we'll never be finished in time for the mayor's visit!"

"We can't let that happen, Rachel," Kirsty whispered to her friend.

"We'll have to work much faster, everyone," Janet called. "Otherwise all our hard work will be concreted over!"

"If only I could find my wand," Edie sighed as everyone got back to work.

"Then I could help to finish the garden with fairy magic."

Rachel frowned. "Where there's mess and trouble and a missing wand, there must be a goblin!" she pointed out.

"Let's find him before he causes any more damage," Kirsty suggested.

Quickly she climbed up onto the back of a nearby truck.
"Come on, Rachel, we can get a good view all over the garden from here!"

Rachel clambered up, too, and the girls looked carefully around the garden. All the volunteers were back at work again, and they couldn't see anything out of the ordinary.

Then Kirsty clutched Rachel's arm.

"Look!" she whispered, "Over there on the edge of the garden, by the biggest rubbish heap!"

Rachel saw a very short person wearing a big, floppy straw hat and oversized overalls. He was sorting through the pile of junk and throwing bits of rubbish right and left, making a mess of the tidy heap.

"Come on!" Rachel murmured, climbing down from the truck.

The girls ran across the garden. As they got closer to the strange-looking gardener, they noticed his big feet and large, pointy ears.

"It's a goblin!" Kirsty said, eyes wide.

Ribbon of Sparkles

"Hurry, girls!" Edie urged them.

Rachel and Kirsty dashed up to the goblin. Luckily he was standing quite far away from the other volunteers, and no one had noticed him.

"Where's Edie's wand?" Rachel demanded, as she and Kirsty cornered the goblin. "We'd like it back, please!"

The goblin gave a shriek of surprise. Then he scowled fiercely as Edie fluttered out of Rachel's pocket.

"Pesky girls!" he muttered. "And a pesky fairy, too. Well, I wouldn't give you the wand, even if I had it."

"What do you mean?" Kirsty asked.

The goblin shrugged. "I've lost it in all the mess I've made!" he muttered sheepishly.

The girls and Edie glanced at each other in dismay.

"The wand could be *anywhere*!" Kirsty groaned.

"Why are you trying to undo all our good work?" Rachel asked the goblin.

"This place is supposed to be green, isn't it?" the goblin asked crossly. "And as I'm the only thing that's *truly* green around here, I get to decide what goes on!" He folded his arms and stared stubbornly at Edie and the girls. "And I like the sound of a nice, smooth car park where I'll be able to roller-skate!"

Edie sighed. "My wand changes itself to fit the person who used it last, so it'll be goblin-sized now," she told the girls. "That means it will be easier to spot.

But we must find it quickly before it falls into human hands. I don't know *what* will happen then!"

"I'm going to find the wand first!" the goblin retorted, and he began pulling the junk heap apart. "I know I last saw it when I was scattering the rubbish around the garden," the goblin mumbled to himself, picking up a battered old radio. He pushed a button, and music began to play.

The goblin looked puzzled. "Why's this been thrown away?" he asked.

"I don't know why people can't put their rubbish where it belongs, and not dump it in the countryside," Rachel said.

"Or they could recycle it," Kirsty added.

The goblin began burrowing into the pile again, tossing bits of junk everywhere. Edie and the girls glared at him.

"We'd better start looking through the other rubbish heaps," Rachel whispered to her friends. "We must find the wand before the goblin does!"

Edie, Rachel and Kirsty moved to a nearby rubbish pile and began searching through the rusty tools, old TV sets and broken bicycles. As Kirsty picked up a crumpled cardboard box, she once again noticed a flash of russet brown from the corner of her eye.

"The fox is back," she thought, turning to look.

Kirsty saw the fox dart towards one of the nearby fields. She blinked. It looked like the fox was leaving behind a ribbon of sparkles as he ran.

"Look!" Kirsty said, pointing out the fox to Rachel and Edie. "Isn't that odd?"

Edie gasped with surprise. "That fox has my wand!" she exclaimed. "He's leaving a trail of fairy magic!" She turned to Rachel and Kirsty. "It'll be quicker if we fly after him, girls – and I have just enough magic of my own to turn you into fairies!"

Edie hovered above Rachel and Kirsty and clapped her hands. A shower of glittering fairy dust floated down onto the girls, and they began to shrink.

Meanwhile, shimmering fairy wings appeared on their shoulders.

"Quick, we mustn't let it get away!" Edie whispered, so that the goblin couldn't hear.

The three friends rose up into the air and flew after the fox, who was now bounding across the field.

"Don't lose sight of him!" Kirsty panted as they zoomed through the air.

Rachel glanced down and cried out in dismay. "The goblin's following us!" she called. "He's worked out that we're on the trail of the wand!"

Which Wand?

"I think the fox has realised that we're following him too!" Kirsty shouted, as the fox ducked smartly into a clump of tall grass, out of sight.

"Don't be scared, Mr Fox," Edie called as the fox reappeared further along the hedgerow and then bolted off again. "We won't hurt you!"

The fox slowed down a little and glanced up at Edie and the girls, waving his brush-like tail to and fro. They could see he had Edie's wand clutched between his teeth.

"Interfering fairies!" the goblin screeched furiously, as he dashed across the field. "Give me back my wand!"

The fox looked very nervous and took off again. He ran right into the middle of a tall bush and disappeared.

"The goblin's scared him away!" Kirsty groaned.

"Where's the wand?" the goblin demanded suspiciously, staring up at the three friends as they hovered over the bush. "Is it in here?"

The goblin began shoving the branches of the bush aside, and suddenly the fox poked his furry head out. The goblin shrieked in triumph as he saw the glittering wand.

"Give that to me!" he shouted, trying to grab it from the fox.

But the fox was too quick for him. He jumped out of the bush and ran off. The goblin lunged after him, but only managed to grab the fox's tail.

The goblin hung on grimly, but the fox managed to wriggle free and throw the goblin off-balance.

"Help!" the goblin screeched as he toppled backwards into the bush. He tried to pull himself out, but he got all tangled up in his outsized overalls. Edie and the girls couldn't help laughing.

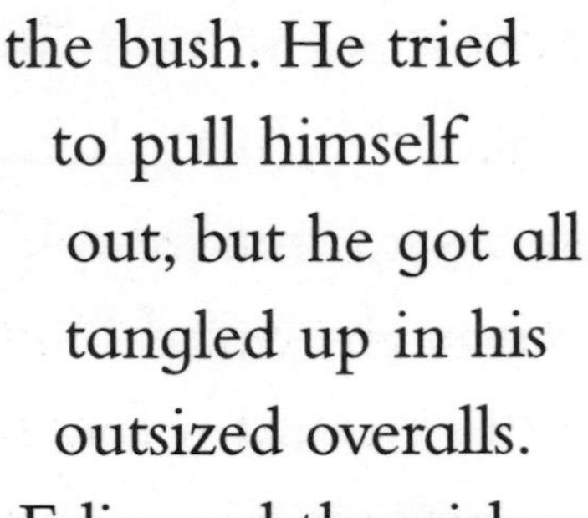

"There's the fox," Rachel whispered.

The fox had stopped a little way off and was staring at the goblin, Edie, Rachel and Kirsty with curiosity. He still had the wand in his mouth.

"If we try to catch the fox, he'll just run off again," Edie said in a low voice.

"We have to persuade him to give us the wand."

"We'd better get rid of the goblin first!" Kirsty pointed out. She glanced at the goblin who was still struggling to untangle himself. "He just keeps scaring the fox away."

"I have an idea!" Edie winked at them. Then she waved her arms in a pretty pattern and a few sparkles of fairy magic appeared. They floated on the breeze across the field. One landed on the grass, and Rachel and Kirsty were then amazed to see two rabbits pop their heads out of a hole.

Another couple of sparkles settled on a nearby tree. The next moment, two squirrels popped their heads out of the leaves.

"Thank you for answering our call for help, my friends!" Edie said, as the squirrels and rabbits gathered round them. "Can you distract that goblin while I use my magic to talk to the fox?"

The rabbits and the squirrel looked at the goblin, who was still trying to untangle himself.

"How?" one of the squirrels asked.

Rachel frowned. She stared down at the long blades of grass around them, and suddenly she had an idea.

"Quick, Edie, make me and Kirsty human-sized again, please!" Rachel said.

Edie nodded and did so.

"Now, Kirsty, help me break off four blades of grass the same size as Edie's wand," Rachel went on.

"Oh, I think I guess what your idea is, Rachel!" Kirsty laughed, as she selected a tall blade of grass.

The girls chose four grass stalks. Then they opened the magic lockets Queen Titania had given them and sprinkled the grass with fairy

dust, so that they shimmered in the sun just like Edie's wand.

"Fake wands!" Edie said with a smile, as the girls handed a blade of grass to each of the rabbits and the squirrels. "What a brilliant idea."

"Now just run off in different directions!" Kirsty whispered to the rabbits and squirrels. They all nodded and then scurried off across the fields.

By now, the goblin had just about managed to scramble to his feet.

"Look!" Rachel shouted, pointing across the fields. "I see the wand!"

"Yes, a squirrel has it!" Kirsty added.

The goblin stopped and glanced around while Kirsty, Rachel and Edie held their breath. Would the goblin be fooled by the fake wands?

"Yah!" the goblin jeered, sticking his tongue out at them. "You can't trick *me!*"

And he pointed in the opposite direction where a rabbit was hopping along, trailing glitter. "That rabbit has the wand!" the goblin yelled. And he chased after it.

"Now we can talk to the fox in peace!" Edie whispered.

The girls walked quietly over to the fox, Edie hovering around them. This time the fox didn't run away.

"Hello," Kirsty said softly. "That wand belongs to our friend Edie the Garden Fairy, and she'd really like it back."

The fox looked stubborn.

"It's mine," he muttered through his teeth. "I found it. Finders keepers!"

"But if Edie gets her wand back, we'll be able to finish the garden," Rachel explained. "If we don't finish, it'll be turned into a car park instead."

"There won't be any flowers or trees,"

Kirsty added. "Just lots and lots of concrete and cement."

The fox frowned. "I don't like that at all," he said slowly. He sat there for a moment, and then he placed the wand on the grass. "Here, take it."

"Oh, thank you!" Edie exclaimed joyfully. She fluttered down and touched the wand, which immediately shrank down to fairy-size.

"You're welcome," the fox replied, bounding away.

Rachel turned as she heard a loud, rumbling sound in the distance. "Here come the diggers!" she gasped.

"That means the mayor must have arrived, too."

Edie and the girls hurried back to the garden. As they went, they saw the rabbits and the squirrels criss-crossing the field in front of the goblin, waving their fake wands. The goblin was chasing first one, then another, looking very hot and bothered.

"I wonder when he'll realise that the animals have pretend wands?" Rachel laughed.

"I'll send him home soon if he doesn't work it out!" Edie replied with a wink.

As the girls reached the garden, the diggers drew up in the lanc. All the volunteers, including Janet, were gathered around the mayor near the wooden arch. But Rachel and Kirsty were dismayed to see that the garden hadn't been finished.

"Don't worry, girls," Edie whispered, ducking out of sight behind Kirsty's hair. "Now I have my wand, I can help!"

Rachel and Kirsty watched eagerly as Edie waved her wand. A mist of glittering fairy dust cleared away all the rubbish in a trice. Another flick of Edie's wand made the flowers bloom just a little more brightly, and also made all the green leaves shine. Then Edie sent a stream of magical sparkles towards the middle of the garden and a large bed of beautiful, multi-coloured flowers appeared.

"Please do come and see what we've done," Janet said to the mayor, as everyone turned to look at the garden. "We didn't have much time, but –" She stopped, looking surprised. "Well, it looks even more beautiful than I thought it did!"

"This is wonderful!" the mayor declared, his face breaking into a smile. "Please show me around, Janet."

"You and all the other volunteers have done a great job," Edie whispered to Kirsty and Rachel, as Janet took the mayor on a tour of the garden.

"Now I have my wand I'm going to take care of all the gardens on Rainspell, and everywhere else!"

"I don't think we need a car park here," the mayor announced with a smile. "I think that this space should definitely be a wildlife garden!"

Rachel and Kirsty cheered and applauded with everyone else as the diggers rumbled away. Edie looked delighted, too.

"I must get back to Fairyland and tell everyone the good news," she murmured.

"Thank you, girls, and remember to keep a look-out for goblins and wands!" And Edie blew them both a kiss and disappeared in a cloud of fairy dust.

"Doesn't it feel good to do something for Rainspell Island, Rachel?" Kirsty said happily. "After all, this is where we met our very first magical friends, the Rainbow Fairies!"

Rachel nodded in agreement.

"What shall we call the park?" the mayor asked Janet.

Janet glanced at the cluster of multi-coloured flowers in the middle. "How about *Rainbow Park?*" she suggested.

Rachel and Kirsty glanced at each other with a smile as everyone cheered.

"Perfect!" Rachel whispered.

Edie the Garden Fairy has got her wand back! Now Rachel and Kirsty must help...

Coral the Reef Fairy

Kirsty Tate beamed as she stepped onto the beach. "This looks *magical*!" she exclaimed, gazing around in excitement.

Her best friend Rachel Walker was close behind. "And there's so much to do," she said, her eyes bright. "Where shall we go first?"

The two girls had come with their parents to Rainspell Beach, where the local surfing group was holding a 'Save the Coral Reefs' event. As Kirsty and Rachel looked around, they could see a crowd of people dancing to the lively beat of a samba band, a line of food stalls which all smelled delicious, games to play, an information centre, surrounded by banners and flags covered in pictures of brightly coloured tropical fish.

"Maybe we should split up and meet back here in an hour for lunch?" Mr Walker, Rachel's dad, suggested.

"Good idea," Rachel replied. "We'll meet you at the information centre at twelve, shall we?" She slipped an arm through Kirsty's. "Come on, let's explore."

The girls made their way into the crowd, enjoying the hustle and bustle of the event. They were here on the island for a week's half-term holiday and so far they'd had a very exciting few days, helping their new fairy friends, the Green Fairies.

"There's another good reason for going off on our own," Kirsty said, thinking about the adventures they'd had lately. "We might meet another fairy, today."

Rachel grinned and held up crossed fingers. "Here's hoping!" she said.

At the start of the week, Kirsty and Rachel had magically transported themselves to Fairyland to ask King Oberon and Queen Titania for their help to clean up the human world. They had met seven fairies-in-training who were each allocated a special mission; when their training was complete, they would become the 'Green Fairies', helping to save the environment in both the human world and Fairyland...

There's nothing like a garden - a special piece of nature that can be planted almost anywhere. It's prettier than a concrete car park, and so much better for the environment! Why not create your own special garden?

Edie the Garden Fairy
xx

Plant your own garden

You will need: seeds or seedlings; soil; water; something to plant your garden in

- Plant a variety of small houseplants in a large pot, window box, or washing-up bowl.
- **For a patio garden:** Choose plants that attract butterflies and other insects, but whose roots don't spread. Plant in large pots, hanging baskets or window boxes.
- **For an outdoor garden:** First draw a plan of your garden showing which plants you'll have where. Include a wildlife area. Also try planting fruits and vegetables for a garden you can eat!

Question:
How many different kinds of plants grow on Earth?
Answer:
About 350,000!

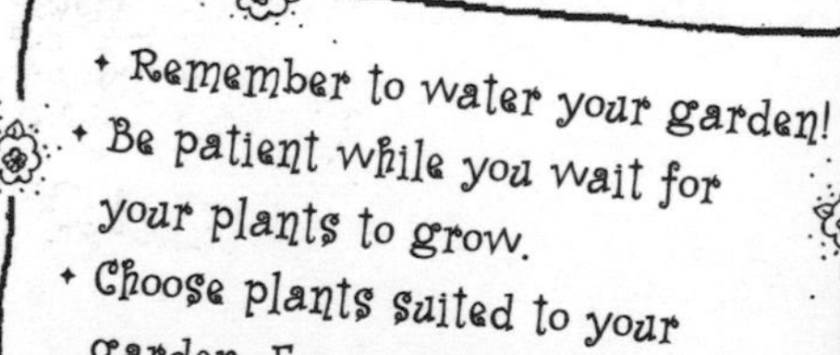

Win Rainbow Magic goodies!

In every book in the Green Fairies series (books 78-84) there is a hidden picture of the Earth with a secret letter in it. Find all seven letters and re-arrange them to make a special Green Fairies word, then send it to us. Each month we will put the entries into a draw and select one winner to receive a Rainbow Magic sparkly T-shirt and goody bag!

Send your entry on a postcard to Rainbow Magic Green Fairies Competition, Orchard Books, 338 Euston Road, London NW1 3BH. Australian readers should write to Hachette Children's Books, Level 17/207 Kent Street, Sydney, NSW 2000.
New Zealand readers should write to Rainbow Magic Competition, 4 Whetu Place, Mairangi Bay, Auckland, NZ. Don't forget to include your name and address. Only one entry per child.
Final draw: 30th September 2010.

Have you checked out the

website at:

www.rainbowmagic.co.uk

Meet the Ocean Fairies in April 2010!

Ally the Dolphin Fairy
978-1-40830-815-8

Amelie the Seal Fairy
978-1-40830-816-5

Pia the Penguin Fairy
978-1-40830-817-2

Tess the Sea Turtle Fairy
978-1-40830-818-9

Stephanie the Starfish Fairy
978-1-40830-819-6

Whitney the Whale Fairy
978-1-40830-820-2

Courtney the Clownfish Fairy
978-1-40830-821-9